Our Beautiful Work of A.R.T.

By Rozanne Nathalie

Illustrations/Graphics
by Jennifer Lofchie and Bruce Sulzberg

Beaver's Pond Press, Inc.
Edina, Minnesota

ISBN 1-931646-76-7

Printed in the United States of America

First Printing: September 2002

06 05 04 03 02   6 5 4 3 2 1

Beaver's Pond Press, Inc.

5125 Danen's Drive
Edina, MN 55439-1465
(952) 829-8818
www.beaverspondpress.com

to order, visit *midwestbookhouse.com* or call
1-877-430-0044. Quantity discounts available.

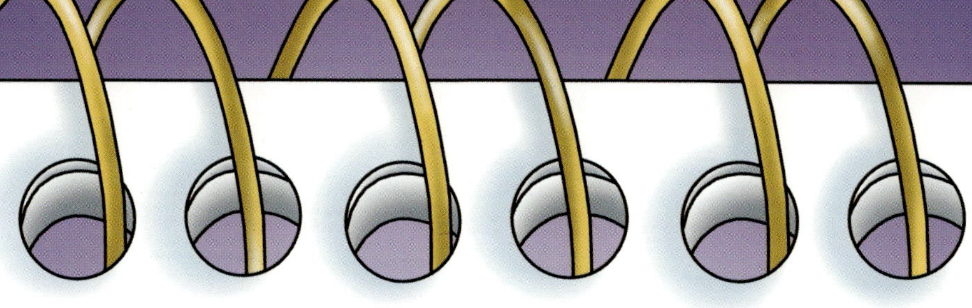

Note from Author

Dear Parents,

I have written these books for you to use as a tool. They are to assist you in explaining to your children the miracle of how they came into your lives. This series was born from 10 years of extraordinary experiences with incredible people such as you. They are truly my labors of love.

I recognize that there are many different, remarkable and beautiful family units that exist; however, for the sake of simplicity these books are written using the traditional "Mommy and Daddy." However, they can easily be adapted to be read with one or the other, by changing "we" to "I," "our" to "my," etc.

This is a keepsake book that your child will treasure as they get older. It will forever remind them of all the love that it took to help them come into this world. Please use the last page of this book to write a letter to your child so that your words of love will be indelibly imprinted in your child's life.

My sincere congratulations,

Rozanne Nathalie

Our Beautiful Work of A.R.T.
By Rozanne Nathalie

Dreams come true when
a baby is born,
But when we tried to have
you our hearts were torn.

Mommy and Daddy had been trying so long,
We had to go to the doctor to see what was wrong.

It shouldn't take so long to make a baby you see,
And Mommy wanted to know "What's wrong with me?"

We had always dreamed
of having you
So we asked the doctor
to help make it come true.

The Doctor was kind and very helpful to us.
He found what was wrong and made plans
with no fuss.

He told us we'd have you but what we need to do
Was follow his plan with the help of his crew.

We were going to work with
a special team
Who knew just what to do to
fulfill our dream.
LABORATORY
WAITING
ROOM
LUNCH
ROOM

We would have to visit the Doctor's spot
And make sure they had all our parts to concoct...

This plan of his that was special indeed,
To combine our parts and make a seed.

This seed was a little You, you know,
And it was carefully put in Mommy to grow.

Little You was perfect. We were full of joy!
What would you be, a girl or a boy?

So there you were growing day by day
Inside my tummy in a special way.
And there you would stay until it was time,
For you to come out and be Daddy's and mine.

You're our very special baby and this is true,
And you're lucky as so many adore you.

It took a whole team to make you, you know
And we all wanted you desperately and love you so.

to baby . . .

As many of your experiences reflect, it takes a collaborative effort of a dedicated team to help make dreams come true . . . and this project is no different. What started as a dream is now a reality thanks to the generous support of Serono Inc., makers of infertility pharmaceuticals. They saw the vision, recognized the need, and worked diligently with me to help bring these books to you. I know that I speak for more than just myself when I say "Thank you Serono."
serono
biotech & beyond

Tell Your Child

Special Stories for Special Children

www.TellYourChild.com